TULSA CITY-COUNTY LIBRARY
5/04
CCER

silly Millies

Bessie's Bed

by Terry Webb Harshman
illustrated by Sharon Hawkins Vargo

The Millbrook Press
Brookfield, Connecticut

For Zachary, who's forever smuggling ferrets into his bed. —T.W.H.

For Judie and pets! —S.H.V.

Copyright © 2003 by Terry Webb Harshman
Illustrations copyright © 2003 by Sharon Hawkins Vargo
All rights reserved

Reading Consultant: Lea M. McGee

Silly Millies and the Silly Millies logo are trademarks of The Millbrook Press, Inc.

Library of Congress Cataloging-in-Publication Data
Harshman, Terry Webb.
Bessie's bed / by Terry Webb Harshman ; illustrated by Sharon Hawkins Vargo.
p. cm. — (Silly Millies)
Summary: On a stormy night, one animal after another knocks at Bessie's door asking for a place to sleep and she always finds room for one more, despite their bad manners.
ISBN 0-7613-2742-8 (lib. bdg.) — ISBN 0-7613-1925-5 (pbk.)
[1. Animals—Fiction. 2. Thunderstorms—Fiction. 3. Behavior—Fiction. 4. Stories in rhyme.] I. Vargo, Sharon Hawkins, ill. II. Title. III. Series.
PZ8.3.H248Be 2003 [E]—dc21 2003000342

Published by The Millbrook Press
2 Old New Milford Road
Brookfield, Connecticut 06804
www.millbrookpress.com

Printed in the United States of America
5 4 3 2 1 (lib.)
5 4 3 2 1 (pbk.)

Bessie's sleeping snug and warm.
But outside there's a dreadful storm.
A sudden knock upon the door
wakes Bessie from her sleepy snore . . .

HOME
SWEET
HOME

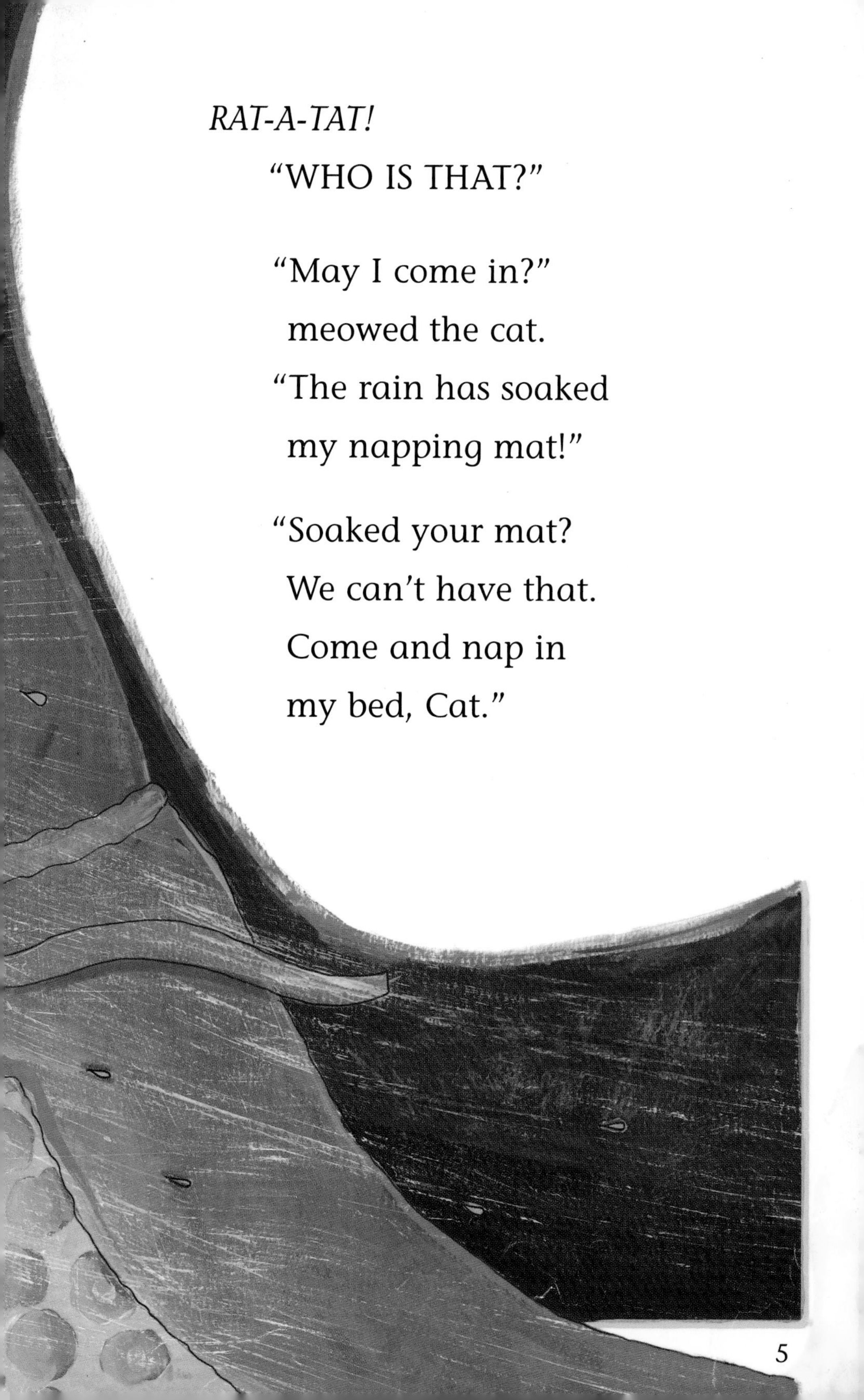

RAT-A-TAT!

"WHO IS THAT?"

"May I come in?"
meowed the cat.
"The rain has soaked
my napping mat!"

"Soaked your mat?
We can't have that.
Come and nap in
my bed, Cat."

“Thank you and good night,”
purred Cat.

He curled up tight
and that was that—
until . . .

HOME
SWEET
HOME

RAT-A-TAT!

"Who is THERE?"

"May I come in?"
begged the bear.
"My lair is leaking
everywhere!"

"A leaking lair?
How dreadful, Bear!
My bed has lots of
room to spare."

So Bear crawled in and growled at Cat,

who spit and spat,

and that was that—

until . . .

HOME
SWEET
HOME

RAT-A-TAT!

"Oh, my—WHO WAKES?"

"May I come in?"
asked the snake.
"My nest has turned
into a lake!"

"Into a lake?
For goodness sake!
Come and nest in
my bed, Snake."

So Snake squeezed in and hissed at Bear,

who growled at Cat,

who spit and spat,

and that was that—

until . . .

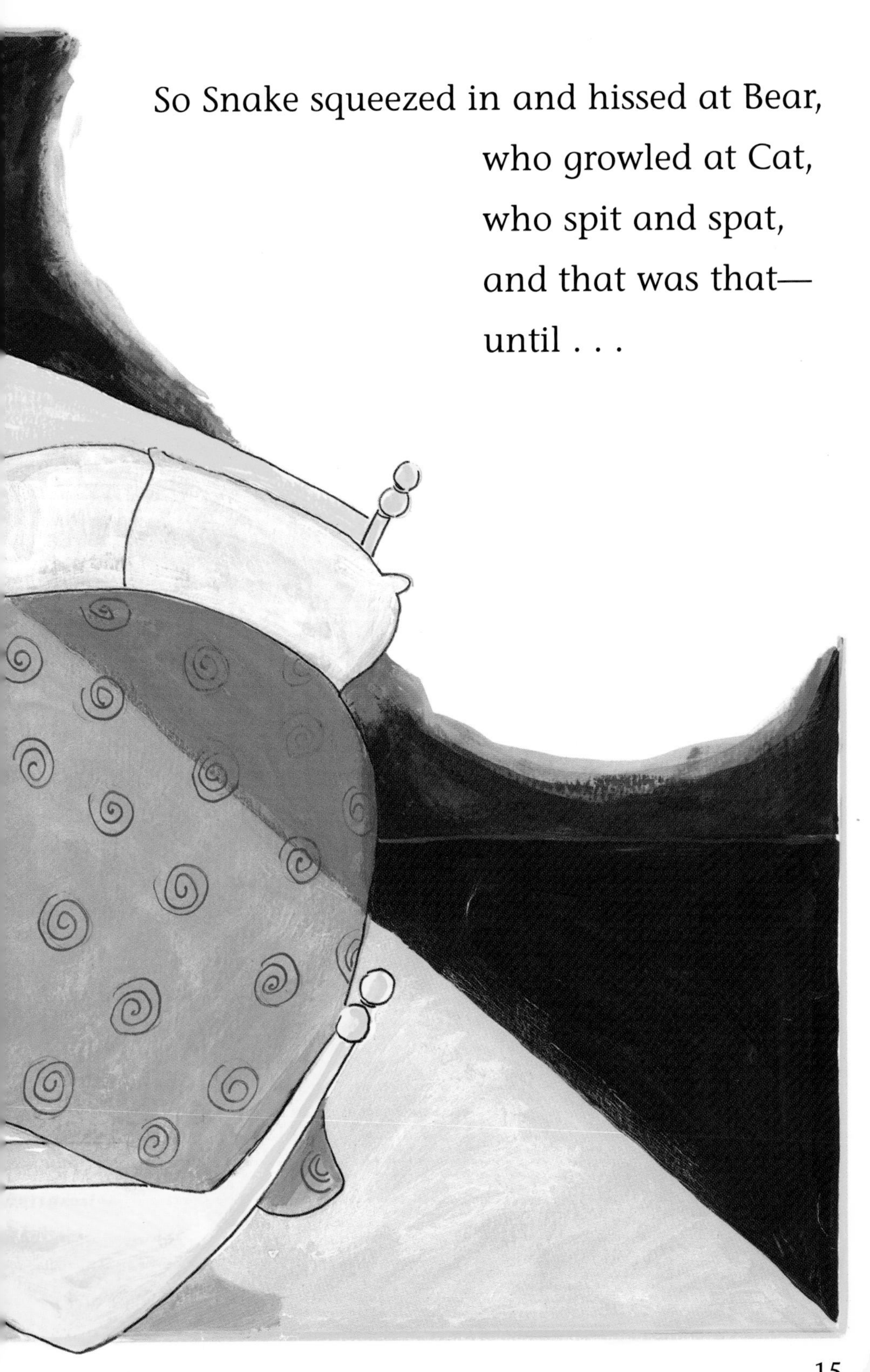

HOME
SWEET
HOME

RAT-A-TAT!

"NOW who knocks?"

"May I come in?"
fretted Fox.
"The rain has blocked
my den with rocks!"

"Blocked with rocks?
Oh, my socks!
You may sleep in
this bed, Fox."

So Fox jumped in and snapped at Snake,

who hissed at Bear,

who growled at Cat,

who spit and spat,

and that was that—

until . . .

HOME
SWEET
HOME

RAT-A-TAT!

"Who can THIS be?"

"May I come in?"
bleated Sheep.
"The barnyard mud
is ankle-deep!"

"Ankle-deep?
Now don't
you weep.
My jumbo bed
can sleep a sheep."

So Sheep climbed in and kicked at Fox,
who snapped at Snake,
who hissed at Bear,
who growled at Cat,
who spit and spat,
and that was that—
until . . .

“That’s quite ENOUGH!” Bessie said.
“You’re all too rude to share my bed!
Behave yourselves and be polite,
or out you’ll go this stormy night!”
Then lightning lit up Bessie’s room
and thunder rumbled—
CRASH! KA-BOOM!

The frightened guests all hid their heads.
"We promise to be good," they said.

No one kicked
or snapped
or hissed
or growled
or spit or spat;
they snuggled up
and that was that—
until . . .

a horrid rumble—
deep and frightening—
worse than thunder—
worse than lightning—
shook the ceiling, bed, and flooring!

Cried the cat,
"It's Bessie SNORING!"
This was more than
they could take.
"Why don't we
move her?"
hissed the snake.

They carried Bessie to the shed
then hurried back to Bessie's bed.

Sheep hopped in and kicked at Fox,
who snapped at Snake,
who hissed at Bear,
who growled at Cat,
who spit and spat,
and . . .

that was that!
(It really was.)

Dear Parents:

Congratulations! By sharing this book with your child, you are taking an important step in helping him or her become a good reader. *Bessie's Bed* is a Level 2 Silly Milly—perfect for children who are beginning to read alone, either silently or aloud. Below are some ideas for making sure your child's reading experience is a positive one.

Tips for Reading

- First, read the book aloud to your child. Then, if your child is able to "sound out" the words, invite him or her to read to you. If your child is unsure about a word you can help by asking, "What word do you think it might be?" or, "Does that make sense?" Point to the first letter or two of the word and ask your child to make that sound. If she or he is stumped, read the word slowly, pointing to each letter as you sound them out. Always provide lots of praise for the hard work your child is doing.
- If your child knows the words but is having trouble reading aloud, cut a plain white ruler-sized strip of paper to place under the line as your child reads. This will help your child keep track of his or her place.
- If your child is a beginning reader, have her or him read this book aloud to you. Reading and rereading is the best way to help any child become a successful reader.

Tips for Discussion

- It is important to search the pictures for clues about words. After you've read the book together a couple of times, ask your child to remember what animal arrives next. See if he or she notices the hint in the window. Another picture clue: Who are the two largest creatures in the bed? How can you tell?
- Ask your child to imagine what noises the animals in this book make. How would he or she spell those noise words?
- The book is a funny story, but it also tells about animal homes. Ask your child what a bear's home is called. A snake's? A fox's? The answers are in the story.

Lea M. McGee, Ed.D.
Professor, Literacy Education,
University of Alabama